Into the ... it goes.

"Man, this porker is awesome," Harry said, setting Sang-ho on his desk. "He stands up, too!" When Harry made *oink oink* noises and snorted, Song Lee giggled.

Within five seconds, Mrs. Bernbotham appeared at Harry's desk.

"I'll take that paper swine now," she said, snatching it from his desk.

"But that pig isn't—"

"Silence!" she snapped.

"—mine," Harry whimpered.

HORRIBLE HARRY
and the June Box

BY SUZY KLINE
PICTURES BY AMY WUMMER

PUFFIN BOOKS
An Imprint of Penguin Group (USA) Inc.

Puffin Books

Published by the Penguin Group

Penguin Young Readers Group, 345 Hudson Street, New York, New York 10014, U.S.A.

Penguin Group (Canada), 90 Eglinton Avenue East, Suite 700, Toronto, Ontario, Canada M4P 2Y3

(a division of Pearson Penguin Canada Inc.)

Penguin Books Ltd, 80 Strand, London WC2R 0RL, England

Penguin Ireland, 25 St Stephen's Green, Dublin 2, Ireland (a division of Penguin Books Ltd)

Penguin Group (Australia), 250 Camberwell Road, Camberwell, Victoria 3124, Australia

(a division of Pearson Australia Group Pty Ltd)

Penguin Books India Pvt Ltd, 11 Community Centre, Panchsheel Park, New Delhi – 110 017, India

Penguin Group (NZ), 67 Apollo Drive, Rosedale, Auckland 0632, New Zealand

(a division of Pearson New Zealand Ltd.)

Penguin Books (South Africa) (Pty) Ltd, 24 Sturdee Avenue,

Rosebank, Johannesburg 2196, South Africa

Penguin Books Ltd, Registered Offices: 80 Strand, London WC2R 0RL, England

First published in the United States of America by Viking,

a division of Penguin Young Readers Group, 2011

Published by Puffin Books, a member of Penguin Young Readers Group, 2012

5 7 9 10 8 6 4

Text copyright © Suzy Kline, 2011

Illustrations copyright © Viking Children's Books, 2011

Illustrations by Amy Wummer

All rights reserved

THE LIBRARY OF CONGRESS HAS CATALOGED THE VIKING EDITION AS FOLLOWS:

Kline, Suzy.

Horrible Harry and the June box / by Suzy Kline ; illustrated by Amy Wummer.

p. cm.

Summary: When the origami pig that Song Lee made for her grandmother is seized by a
substitute teacher, the usually well-behaved third-grader breaks a classroom rule to rescue
it from the "June box."

ISBN 978-0-670-01265-7 (hardcover)

[1. Substitute teachers—Fiction. 2. Schools—Fiction. 3. Behavior—Fiction.]

I. Wummer, Amy, ill. II. Title.

PZ7.K6797Hnoj 2011 [Fic]—dc22 2011001503

Puffin Books 978-0-14-242185-7

Set in New Century Schoolbook

Printed in the United States of America

ALWAYS LEARNING   PEARSON

To my handsome grandson, Jake,
who is a wonderful mathematician.
I love you!
Grandma Sue. —S.K.

To Brianna, who read the story
with me on the beach! —A.W.

Special appreciation for the people who inspired this story:

Teachers who use a June box in their classroom; Mark Twain's *Tom Sawyer* and his wonderful Chapter 20; my neighbor, dear friend, and math teacher, Lisa Finkleman, who told me about Gauss; my lovable husband, Rufus, who came up with the names Bernbotham and Goolavoomba and helped me with the first draft; and especially my perceptive editors, Catherine Frank and Leila Sales, whose help was invaluable.

Contents

The June Box

My name is Doug, and I'm in third grade. I write stories about my friend Harry, who loves horrible, creepy things. Sometimes he even makes scary creatures out of pencil stubs, paper clips, dirty eraser bits, and broken crayons. Harry calls them stub people. Last year he used them to stage an invasion in Room 2B. Nowadays, most of his men wind up in the teacher's June box.

What's a June box, you ask?

It's a jail for toys.

Ours is made of wood and big enough to hold a football. It sits on top of the teacher's desk. Miss Mackle keeps a small, prickly cactus plant on top of it.

Sidney calls it a maximum security prison for his canary stickers.

Mary thinks it's a good idea. "You shouldn't be fooling around with stuff when the teacher is talking. It's a distraction. You should be doing your work."

Harry is counting the days until the end of school. That's when Miss Mackle will open up the June box and give him back his stub people. "I miss Radio Man the most. His buttons come from my great granddad's army shirt from World War II. They're made of metal and have an eagle on them. They make the coolest radio dials. Radio Man is the general of my stub people. I can't have another invasion without him. Ninety-six days!"

"I miss my Elvis bobblehead," Dexter complains. "I was just humming 'Blue Suede Shoes' and making him shuffle sideways on my desk, but the teacher took him anyway."

So far, those guys are the only ones in Room 3B who have stuff in Miss Mackle's June box.

I *never* thought that Song Lee would, too. Not in a million years! But it happened, and it catapulted Harry to his worst doom!

It all started on the last Monday morning in February.

Harry and I were walking down the school ramp.

"*Look!*" Harry yelled. "The snow and ice are finally gone! Do you know what that means, Doug?"

"OUTDOOR RECESS!" we both shouted. It seemed like ages since our last kickball game. Harry and I leaped into the air.

At that moment, Mr. Beausoleil, our custodian, pulled up in front of the school in his pickup truck. When he walked down the ramp, he had two huge duffel bags slung over his shoulder.

"Are you Santa Claus?" Harry joked.

Mr. Beausoleil chuckled. "Well, I do have gifts!" He set the bags down and

opened one of them. Harry and I moved
closer as he pulled back the drawstrings.
Other kids gathered around. They were
curious, too.

"KICKBALLS!" we all shouted.

Harry pressed his nose on one of them. "Mmmmmmmm. My favorite smell! Red rubber. Man, this kickball is filled with lots of air!" Harry patted it gently, like he was burping a baby.

Mary came over, rolling her eyes. "Just new kickballs?"

Mr. Beausoleil opened up the other bag.

"JUMP ROPES!" Mary, Ida, and

Song Lee squealed. Sidney cheered, too. Those four love chanting songs while they jump rope.

The custodian scooped up the bags and headed toward the building. "You guys will get your new equipment in time for noon recess today. The weatherman says, 'cool but clear.'"

"I get to jump first," Sid called out.

"I'm second," Mary replied.

"Song Lee and I get to turn the jump rope," Ida insisted.

The girls were bouncing up and down.

"Noon recess is gonna be heaven," Harry said, slapping everyone five.

"Yeah!" ZuZu, Dexter, and I agreed.

"Dibs on being pitcher!" I said.

"I'm up first," Harry exclaimed. "I'm

kicking that red rubber ball to the moon!"

Everyone entered the school building in a great mood.

But when we got to Room 3B and saw who was at Miss Mackle's desk, we all came to a halt.

The Sub

"Mrs. Bernbotham!" Ida whispered. "She's the meanest substitute teacher on the planet! My brother told me all about her."

"Why isn't it Mr. Flaubert?" I said. "He was our last sub. He was nice and fun."

"He sure was!" ZuZu agreed. "We got to do animal projects."

"Hey," Harry replied. "We've got *out-*

Mrs.
Bernbotham

side recess today! Remember? We can deal with any sub."

Dexter rolled his eyes. "Well, this one scares me. She looks six feet tall in those high heels. Just look at her. She has yellow teeth and blue fingernails."

"We'd better hang up our coats, guys," ZuZu said.

Mary was the first to do so. "I think I'll like her. I bet she doesn't let anybody get away with anything. Our room will be nice and quiet for working."

The rest of us made a face as we hung up our jackets and trudged to our desks.

At nine o'clock, the bell rang.

"What's wrong with Miss Mackle?" Harry blurted out.

"When you raise your hand," Mrs.

Bernbotham snapped, "I'll answer that question."

Harry raised his hand. "What's wrong with Miss Mackle?"

"I haven't called on you yet," she replied, checking the seating chart on a clipboard. As she moved her finger down the page, she was able to spot his last name. "Mr. Spooger. Now I'm busy reading the rules and procedures Miss Mackle has listed for Room 3B."

I noticed the sub looked up and patted the June box a few times. That jailhouse was probably listed under consequences.

While Harry kept his hand raised in the air, the sub finally went to the front of the room and introduced herself.

"I'm Mrs. Bernbotham, your substitute teacher. Miss Mackle is at a teacher's conference." Then she wrote something in yellow chalk on the board.

What is the sum of all the numbers from 1 to 100?

Are you kidding? I thought. *How in the world am I going to solve that?*

The sub must have read my mind, because she turned around and said, "I suggest you add up these numbers in pairs and look for a pattern. It will save

you a lot of work. Please copy the question and get busy."

I still didn't understand, but I got out
my math journal anyway.

So did everyone else except Harry.

He still had his hand raised. He

was tapping his fingers in the air like he was playing the piano. "Is Miss Mackle coming back tomorrow?" he called out.

Mrs. Bernbotham shot Harry a look. It said, *Get busy!*

Song Lee took out her math journal. She also took out a small box from her backpack. When she opened it up and showed me the contents, I said, *"Wow!"*

Sang-ho

"It's a pig," she whispered, handing it to me.

Song Lee had made it out of pink origami paper.

"Pigs are good luck in Korea," she said. "It took me five tries to fold it right."

Then she pulled out four other pink paper pigs. One didn't have a tail. One didn't have a snout. Two were half folded and ripped. She shook her head as she stuffed them into her desk.

"Looks like a lot of work," I said, cradling the pig gently.

"About three hours," Song Lee admitted. "I can't wait to send it to Grandma Bong. It's her sixtieth birthday. Mom is mailing it to Korea with my homemade card after school today."

"It looks just like a pig," I replied. "I love the way you folded his ears and curly tail."

"I named him Sang-ho," said Song Lee, chuckling. "After a famous Korean soccer player."

"Cool! That's fun to say. 'Sang-ho,'" I repeated.

Harry finally gave up and put his hand down. "Can I see your pig?" he asked Song Lee.

When she nodded, I passed Sang-ho to Harry. "Just for a minute," she whispered. "I have to put him back in his box and do my math."

"Man, this porker is awesome," Harry said, setting Sang-ho on his desk. "He stands up, too!" When Harry made *oink oink* noises and snorted, Song Lee giggled.

Within five seconds, Mrs. Bernbotham appeared at Harry's desk.

"Are you working on your morning math?" she demanded. "Hmmm?"

Harry made a face. He hadn't started.

"I'll take that paper swine now," she said, snatching it from his desk.

Harry objected right away. "But that pig isn't—"

"*Silence!*" she snapped.

"—mine," Harry whimpered.

I don't think she heard him.

Everyone watched Mrs. Bernbotham clomp back to her desk, remove the cactus plant, and open the lid of the June box. She dropped Sang-ho inside, then rubbed her hands together. "I love June boxes!" she said. "They help teach a very valuable lesson."

Her eyes got bigger, and her voice got louder. "NO TOYS IN CLASS!"

Harry sank down in his chair.

Mary and Ida folded their hands.

Sidney and Dexter got busy with their math.

There was nothing anyone could do.

I looked over at Song Lee. She had her head bowed and appeared to be working on her math challenge. But I could see tears falling. They made wet splotches on her math paper.

Mrs. Bernbotham suddenly appeared at Song Lee's desk with a Kleenex. "Is something the matter?" she asked in a low voice.

Song Lee didn't say a word. She just shook her head.

The UNbelievable Happens!

At exactly ten minutes after nine, Mr. Cardini, our principal, made a morning announcement over the intercom. "Boys and girls, each classroom will be getting a new kickball and jump rope. I'm happy to announce that after two long weeks of indoor recess, you will be going outside today. Teachers, when it's convenient for you, please stop by the office and sign out your equipment."

Everyone at South School burst into

cheers. I could hear the other rooms yelling through our open door.

Song Lee wasn't cheering though. She was wiping her tears away with her sweater sleeve.

Mrs. Bernbotham headed for the door. "Boys and girls, I will be right back. I'm going to the office. When I return in two minutes, I expect everyone to be in his or her seat working on our math challenge."

As soon as she stepped into the hallway, the unbelievable happened. Someone popped out of their chair.

It wasn't Harry.

And it wasn't Sidney.

It was *Song Lee*. She was carrying something in her left hand.

She moved so quickly and quietly,

only a few people noticed. Just about everyone was busy adding up numbers. Especially Mary. Her nose was two inches from her paper.

But Harry and I sure saw her. Where was Song Lee going?

To the pencil sharpener?

To get a drink?

When she stopped at the teacher's desk, my mouth dropped open.

Without making any noise, Song Lee moved the prickly cactus plant and opened up the June box!

Suddenly there was the sound of high heels clicking down the hall.

It was Mrs. Bernbotham! Boy, was she a fast walker.

Song Lee quickly closed the lid, then raced back to her desk.

Mary, Ida, Dexter, ZuZu, and Sidney now looked up.

Had Song Lee rescued Sang-ho? I don't think anyone knew for sure what happened.

Song Lee got to her chair just as the sub entered the room. I noticed Song Lee put both of her hands into her backpack, but I couldn't see what she was doing.

"I have your new kickball and jump rope," Mrs. Bernbotham announced as she entered the room. "I hope you know how fortunate you are to have such fine P.E. equipment. Please take good care of it."

While the sub opened the closet and placed the equipment inside our recess box, Mary turned around to Song Lee and pointed to the cactus plant. It was not on the June box. It was on the teacher's desk! Mary kept trying to get Song Lee's attention. It needed to be put back on the box.

Mrs. Bernbotham closed the closet door, then scanned the classroom with her glaring eyes. As soon as she saw Mary gesturing wildly, the sub stopped in her tracks.

When Mary turned around and saw the sub staring at her, she froze.

Mrs. Bernbotham walked over to the teacher's desk and examined it carefully.

"Apparently someone has been tampering with my desk. The cactus plant is not in its proper place."

No one said a word.

Harry's Doom

Mrs. Bernbotham put both hands on our wooden June box. Everyone could see her four flashy rings. One bloody red stone was as big as a nickel.

Oh no! I thought. *She's going to look inside.* Did Song Lee take Sang-ho?

Harry and I held our breath.

The sub opened the lid and eyed the contents of the June box. "Everything seems to be here," she said. "Elvis, canary stickers, that pink pig . . ."

You could hear Harry and me exhale.

It was one giant sigh of relief!

Song Lee didn't have enough time to rescue Sang-ho.

"What are these horrible pencil creatures?" the sub continued. "There must be a dozen of them."

"Those are Harry's stub people," Sid volunteered.

Mrs. Bernbotham cringed, then closed the lid and replaced the cactus plant on top.

I shook my head. What a close call for Song Lee.

The sub reached for the clipboard with the laminated seating chart. "I would like to know," she said, "*who* tampered with the prickly cactus. It's obviously somebody who was out of their seat and not doing math!"

All of us shuddered.

Mrs. Bernbotham moved to the first row. She called us by our last names.

"Miss Burrell," she said. "Did you move the plant?"

"N-n-no," Ida stuttered.

"Mr. LaFleur?" the sub asked. "Did you do it?"

"No way, José!" Sid replied.

"My name is Mrs. Bernbotham," she snapped. "Not José."

Sidney nodded his head multiple times like Dexter's bobblehead Elvis.

The sub lowered her eyebrows as she moved to row two.

It was Song Lee's row. Harry and I were in row three.

"Miss Berg?"

"Oh no, I always follow the rules, Mrs. Bernbotham," Mary answered politely.

The sub was just two desks away from Song Lee's.

"Mr. Hadad?"

"I did not touch the prickly plant," ZuZu said firmly.

"Mr. Sanchez?"

"No, ma'am," Dexter answered. He didn't look up.

The sub was now standing over Song Lee's desk.

"Miss Park," she said. "Did you get out of your seat and move the plant?"

Song Lee very slowly opened her mouth. Her whole body was shaking. Her voice even trembled. "I . . . I . . ."

Before she got to the third "I," Harry jumped up. "I did it!" he said.

Mrs. Bernbotham stepped across the aisle to Harry's desk. "You removed the cactus?"

"Yes."

"Why, Mr. Spooger?"

Harry reached into his desk and pulled out one of his stub people. It had two antennas made out of paper clips stuck into a dirty eraser. Harry had made fangs out of straws.

"I wanted to get TV Man out of the June box," he fibbed.

Mrs. Bernbotham seized TV Man out of Harry's hand. "This creature doesn't deserve to be saved in a June box. I'm tossing him in the garbage where he belongs."

We all watched the sub walk over to the wastepaper basket and drop TV Man inside. She picked up two corners of the white plastic garbage bag and tied them together. "I will personally toss this into the Dumpster myself."

Harry looked shocked.

"In addition, Mr. Spooger," the sub continued, "you will spend lunch and noon recess indoors with me."

That was the killer.

Harry's sentence was the worst. He was going to miss the first outdoor recess in two weeks. No kickball game for him. He wasn't going to kick that brand-new red rubber ball to the moon.

Harry bonked his head down on his desk.

Song Lee looked very sad.

"Now that I've gotten to the bottom of that ill-advised caper, everyone can get back to their math challenge," Mrs Bernbotham snapped.

Harry was doomed.

The Math Challenge

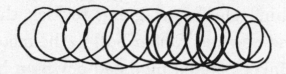

For the next twenty minutes, it was very quiet. Everyone was busy adding except Song Lee and Harry. Song Lee was writing a note. Harry was making circular scribbles that looked like a troop of Slinkys marching across his math journal.

"This problem is going to take forever," Sidney complained.

"I've messed up three times now," Dexter whined.

Mrs. Bernbotham heard our grumblings and went to the blackboard. "Boys and girls," she said, "I want to tell you a story about a very famous German mathematician. His name was Johann Carl Friedrich Gauss. His last name has the same 'ow' sound as cow. *Gauss*. When he was in elementary school, his teacher got mad at the class and ordered them to add the numbers from one to one hundred. Thirty seconds later, much to the surprise of the teacher, Gauss arrived at the correct answer. He used a pattern to solve the very problem you are working on right now. I'm going to show you part of it. It's up

$$1 + 100 = 101$$
$$2 + 99 = 101$$
$$3 + 98 = 101$$

to you to complete Gauss's pattern."

The sub started to pair up numbers on the board.

Suddenly, the fire alarm went off.

Bzzz! Bzzz! Bzzz!

"Single file, no talking," Mrs. Bernbotham ordered. We quickly lined up at the door. Mrs. Bernbotham grabbed the attendance book off her desk, then snatched the white garbage bag on her way out. She led our line briskly down the hall, through the double doors, and out toward the playground. Song Lee and I were at the end of the line with Harry. Just ahead of us were Sid, ZuZu, Mary, and Ida.

"This is the first fire drill we've had in a month," Sid whispered.

"The weather's been too icy to have one," ZuZu replied.

As we marched out to the fence, Mary made a point of getting Harry's attention. *"Pssst!"* she whispered. "Ask Song Lee why she moved the plant."

Harry didn't bother passing her question on. He answered it. "She was

checking on the plant. Didn't you see it had a yellowish disease?"

Mary shook her head. "No. What disease?"

"It's called something like Goola-voomba," Harry answered.

"Goolavoomba? Puhleese . . ." Mary whispered back. "That sounds like the name of a horrible monster."

Ida covered her mouth. She didn't want the sub to hear her laughing.

"Well, disease *is* like a monster," Harry said. "You know how Song Lee cares about every living thing. She just wanted to check on the plant. She took it off the June box to take a closer look."

Mary groaned. It sounded iffy, but Song Lee would do something like that.

Ida gave Harry a smile. "You were very brave to take the blame for Song Lee."

"Or dumb," Mary added.

Harry just shrugged.

When we passed the open Dumpster,

Mrs. Bernbotham heaved the garbage sack over her shoulder. Harry closed his eyes. I knew he was having a moment of silence for TV Man.

As soon as we got to the fence and everyone was being shushed, Song Lee passed Harry a note. I looked over his shoulder and watched him un-fold it. The note was written in neat cursive.

Dear Harry,

I feel bad. It's not fair. I want you to have outdoor recess. I'm telling Mrs. B about Sang-ho.

Your friend always,
Song Lee

Harry stuffed the note into his back pocket and then turned to Song Lee. "Hey," he whispered. "It's my fault. I made those stupid noises that got the sub's attention. Your pig *never* would have ended up in that June box if it wasn't for me."

Harry pointed to the Dumpster. "Do you want your pink pig to end up like TV Man? If you tell the whole truth, that's what will happen. She'll yank Sang-ho out of the June box and toss him in the garbage."

Song Lee looked over at the Dumpster and cringed. "That's not going to happen," she whispered back.

Harry started to say something, but Mrs. Bernbotham was patrolling our end of the line.

"Shhhh!" the sub shushed. "It's a fire drill. No talking!"

When we got back to the room, lots of kids were still grumbling about the hard math problem. I was moaning because Harry was going to miss the coolest recess of third grade! Mary kept erasing her math work and starting over again. ZuZu was making big sighs. Dexter was tapping his pencil on his desk.

"Class," she said. "It's good to be challenged, but I can see many of you are getting frustrated, so I guess I'm going to have to do what *everyone* else does these days—offer a reward."

The sub held up one finger. "If . . . you can get the correct answer to the math challenge by one o'clock, you will get a reward of your choice."

ZuZu raised his hand.

"Yes, Mr. Hadad."

"What do you mean?"

"You get to choose your reward, within reason of course," Mrs. Bernbotham answered.

Everyone sat up and paid attention.

"If it were me," the sub continued, "I would ask for a special trip to the library, check out a new book, and read it right there in a comfortable chair. That would be my reward."

"Could my reward be extra computer time?" ZuZu asked.

"Good choice," Mrs. Bernbotham replied.

"Could you get something out of the June box?" Dexter asked.

Mrs. Bernbotham thought about it. "That's also doable."

"*Yes!*" five of us exclaimed.

If Song Lee, Harry, or I got the answer, we could spring Sang-ho!

Dexter could spring bobblehead Elvis.

And Sid could get his hands on his yellow canary stickers.

Mary and Ida didn't even know about Sang-ho. They thought the paper pig was Harry's. "We could do a craft!" they exclaimed.

"*Shhhh!*" Harry snapped. "I need to concentrate on my math."

Ida and Mary looked surprised. Harry had never shushed them before.

Mrs. Bernbotham smiled for the first time that day. And that's when I saw her four gold capped teeth.

Everyone was working quietly on that math challenge now.

Noontime Recess

Later that morning, we had reading and writing, and then the music teacher came. Twenty minutes before lunch, Mrs. Bernbotham let us continue working on the math challenge.

"I got it!" Sid blurted out.

Mrs. Bernbotham didn't scold him for his outburst. She went over to his desk and checked his answer. "Nice try, Mr. LaFleur," she said. "Keep working."

The sub checked ZuZu's answer and Dexter's and Mary's, too. But they were all wrong.

Harry was working so hard on his math, he was drooling on his paper.

When Song Lee raised her hand, Mrs. Bernbotham rushed over to her. "You're so close!" she exclaimed. "Your pattern is a little bit different from Gauss's, but it will work. Don't give up."

Three minutes later, the bell rang.

Bzzzzzzzzzzzzzzzzzzzzzz!

Harry sank down in his chair. "I'm only half done," he complained.

"Okay, boys and girls," Mrs. Bernbotham said. "Line up for lunch. Mr.

Spooger, you may get your lunchbox and eat at your seat."

"Can I work on my math while I eat?" Harry asked.

"Of course," the sub answered.

I gave Harry two thumbs up. Maybe he could earn Sang-ho back.

As we lined up at the door for lunch, I noticed Song Lee had her math journal tucked under her arm.

After we finished eating, we raced outside for recess. ZuZu, Dexter, and I started up a kickball game with some other kids. When it was my turn to be up, I kicked the ball into left field. It bounced all the way to the fence. As I rounded the bases, I saw Mary and Ida turning the rope for Sid. I didn't see Song Lee.

Dexter was waiting for me when I touched home plate. "YOU ROCK, BABY!" he shouted. Then Dex, Zuzu, and I slapped one another five.

"Too bad Harry isn't here." I groaned.

"Yeah," Dex agreed.

I glanced back at the jump roping. I still didn't see Song Lee.

I wondered where she was.

"I'm getting a quick drink," I said to ZuZu. He was up next.

As I ran to the water fountain, I

stopped by and asked Mary, "Where's Song Lee?"

Mary was still twirling the rope. "Song Lee told me she wanted to work on that math problem, but I don't know where she went. Probably a quiet place."

A quiet place on the playground? Where was that?

I had to get back to my kickball game. Our team was outfield now, so I raced back to the pitcher's mound.

Ten minutes later, the bell rang to go inside. We all headed for the double doors. As I passed the Dumpster, I spotted two pink tennis shoes with butterflies sticking out from behind the dumpster. It was *Song Lee*!

I darted over to her. She was just getting up. She held her math journal close to her heart. "I think I got that math challenge," she whispered.

"You've been doing math all recess?" I asked.

She nodded.

"Whoa," I said.

"I want that special reward."

I walked slowly over to the door. I wanted to keep our conversation private.

"Sure you do. You're going to get Sang-ho back!" I exclaimed.

Song Lee didn't say another word. She just looked very hopeful.

The Awesome Reward!

When we got back to Room 3B, Harry was drooped over his desk, pooped.

I could see he had done more math work than eating. His Ants on a Log and oatmeal cookies were untouched in his lunchbox.

He looked like his cat, the Goog, had died.

I didn't ask him if he got the answer. I knew just by looking at him.

Song Lee immediately went up and showed the sub her notebook.

"You got it!" Mrs. Bernbotham exclaimed. She shot her hands in the air like she was guarding the tallest basketball player. *"Yahoo!"* she called out. Then she gave Song Lee a big hug.

Who was this crazy math lady?

We all clapped loudly for Song Lee.

"Song Lee," Mrs. Bernbotham said. "Please go to the board and show the class how you got the correct answer."

I could tell the sub was in a good mood. She was using Song Lee's first name.

Song Lee glanced at her math journal, then started writing equations. "I paired the numbers a little differently than Gauss did. I started with zero plus one hundred. I made the pairs all equal one hundred. It was easier to add. I found fifty pairs of numbers that total one hundred. That equals five thousand. Then there is one number left over: fifty. So the answer is five thousand fifty."

$$0 + 100 = 100$$
$$1 + 99 = 100$$
$$2 + 98 = 100$$

$$50 \times 100 = 5000$$
$$5000 + 50 = 5050$$

"Whoa," I said. "That's cool!"

"The coolest!" ZuZu agreed.

Dexter and Sidney tried to smile. But they were disappointed they didn't get a reward.

When Song Lee took her seat, Mrs. Bernbotham went to the board. "But the joy of math continues," she said. "Look at the answer, five thousand fifty." And she wrote it on the board again.

5050

"If you do a karate chop on the answer like this"—we all watched the sub hit the blackboard with the side of her hand—"you can separate the two fifties and add them up."

$$50 + 50$$

"Their sum is one hundred, which is the sum of any one of Song Lee's pairs."

$$50 + 50 = 100$$

Lots of us cheered. That was amazing!

"Now, Song Lee," Mrs. Bernbotham

said. "What special reward do you want? You certainly have earned it."

"First, I have to tell you the horrible truth," she said.

Mrs. Bernbotham looked confused. "Excuse me?" she replied.

Oh boy, I thought.

Song Lee sat up straight and spoke clearly. "I was the one who moved the cactus. I was the one who opened up the June box. That pink origami pig was mine. I made it for Grandma Bong. It's her sixtieth birthday and that is very special in Korea. It took me five tries and three hours to make it. Mom was going to mail it right after school. I didn't have time to make another one. Harry took the blame for me. He didn't want my pig to end up in the Dumpster like his TV Man. I should have told you all this before. I am so sorry."

Mrs. Bernbotham tapped her fingers together.

It was pin quiet.

No one could believe that Song Lee would do something like that!

Harry was the first to speak up. "But if I hadn't made *oink oink* noises, that pink pig wouldn't have been a distraction. It really was my fault, Mrs. Bernbotham. Not Song Lee's."

"So . . . you took the pig, Song Lee?" Mrs. Bernbotham asked.

"Yes," she replied.

The sub walked back to her desk and removed the cactus plant. She opened up the June box and held up a pink

paper pig. "What is this then?" she asked.

"One of the pigs I botched up," Song Lee explained. "I switched pigs."

So that's what she had in her hand! I thought.

Ida silently clapped for Song Lee under her desk.

Dexter and Sidney had their mouths wide open.

Harry punched the air.

Mary turned around and glared at Harry. *"Goolavoomba!"* she said in disgust.

Mrs. Bernbotham rolled her eyes. "Well," she sighed. "It's never too late to tell the truth. I'm so glad you did, Song Lee and Harry. Had I known that pig was a special birthday present and you were just showing it to Harry, I would have simply asked you to put it away. And Harry, I would have just asked you to stop making silly noises."

Then Mrs. Bernbotham added, "I remember now that Harry was trying to tell me something about that pig and I wasn't in the mood to listen. So I could have handled things better, too, and I would have known why Song Lee was so upset this morning."

"Does Song Lee still get a special reward?" ZuZu asked. "She solved the math challenge."

"I hope to keep my pig," Song Lee requested, holding up the box she was keeping Sang-ho in.

Mrs. Bernbotham smiled. "I want you to keep your pig. I'm so glad you told the truth and apologized. I would say we had a huge miscommunication this morning. I'm delighted the truth cleared it all up. But that doesn't count as your reward for your wonderful math work. Is there something else you would like?"

Song Lee thought about it, then whispered something in the sub's ear.

When Mrs. Bernbotham nodded yes, Song Lee got out of her seat and walked up to the teacher's desk.

What was she going to do, I wondered?

She opened up the June box, took something out, and held it up.

Radio Man!

Harry's eyes popped out of his sockets.

Song Lee walked over to his desk and handed it to him. "This is for you, Harry," she said, placing it in his two palms. "Thank you for being my friend."

Harry stared at his commanding

general. It was a large dirty eraser with two gold button dials and paper clip antennas. Two broken brown crayons were his legs.

"I'm bringing you home, Radio Man," he said. "What an awesome reward!"

Then he kissed each of the eagle buttons. "Thanks, Song Lee. You're the best."

Song Lee beamed.

Mary continued to frown at Harry. "Goolavoomba," she mumbled.

Harry just flashed a toothy smile.

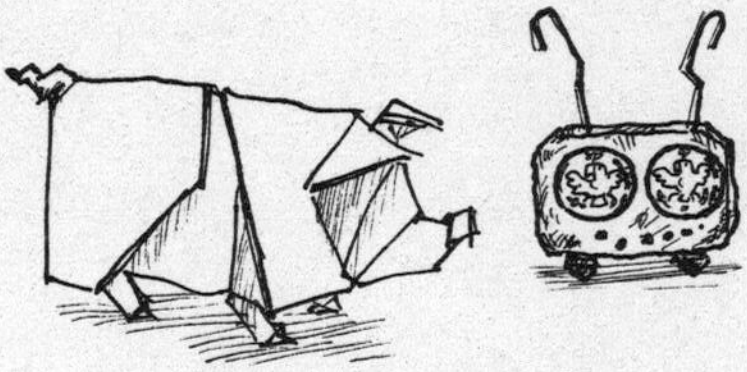